I0623469

ECHOES OF THE FORSAKEN PATH

A Darkspire Chronicles Adventure

Book Two

JPS Nagi

For more information, or to book an event, contact :
Author@JPSNagi.com
http://www.PlanetNagi.com

Book design by JPS Nagi
Cover design by JPS Nagi

ISBN – Paperback: 978-1-966767-07-7
ISBN – eBook: 978-1-966767-08-4

First Edition: January 2026
Library of Congress Control Number: 2025923913

To my children, Khushi & Danish –

Imagination first takes root in the wonder of fairy tales. It is in those stories that dreams grow wings, and the ordinary world becomes extraordinary.

Here is one such tale that I wrote – for you, and for the adventures your own imaginations will one day create.

AUTHOR'S NOTE

Stories, at their heart, are echoes. They ripple outward from a single moment – a choice, a question, a fragment of wonder – and continue long after the moment itself has passed. The *Darkspire Chronicles* were born from this belief: that every tale is both its own song and a thread in a greater harmony.

This series does not follow a single hero or a single prophecy. Instead, it gathers voices from across Thaloria – rangers, clerics, dwarves, sorcerers, and the countless others who live between the cracks of kingdoms and temples. Some stumble into peril unwillingly, others chase after it by choice, but all of them discover that the paths we call "ordinary" are often the ones that shape legends.

Each volume of the *Darkspire Chronicles* is designed to stand on its own, a full tale with its own beginning and end. Yet, together, they form a cycle – a chorus of stories bound by recurring themes: the lure of shadow, the weight of faith, the resilience of companionship, and the simple, enduring power of choice.

These are not stories of grand destinies imposed by gods. They are stories of people who choose, and in choosing, alter not just their fates but the world around them.

If you hear those echoes in these pages – faint but insistent – then you walk with me in this world, and the Chronicles have done their work.

Book Two: *Echoes of Forsaken Paths*

The *Darkspire Chronicles* live in the space between light and shadow – in the questions that rise when faith collides with doubt, when power whispers promises, and when companionship is the only thing standing between ruin and survival. With each volume, the series explores not just the landscapes of Thaloria but the inner landscapes of those who walk its forsaken paths.

This second tale, *Echoes of Forsaken Paths*, holds a special place in the cycle. Where the first story opened the gates into this world, this one carries us deeper into its hidden chambers. Here we find a burned cart smoldering on a lonely road, an inn torn open by sudden magic, and a cavern where every sound is a threat. We step into Everspring, a town divided by temples, where faith threatens to fracture into rivalry. And at the heart of it all, we face revelations that bind bloodlines to villainy, forcing one companion to confront the shadow not of an enemy, but of kin.

These companions – Kaelen, Serenya, Bram, and Lyraen – did not begin their journey as heroes. They are flawed, uncertain, even reluctant. Yet in their doubts and choices lies the truth of this series. The *Darkspire Chronicles* are not about crowns or prophecies. They are about ordinary travelers who find themselves at crossroads no one else dares to walk, and who discover that legends are not born – they are chosen.

Writing this story reminded me of a truth I return to often: adventures live twice. They live first in the immediacy of discovery, when danger and wonder unfold step by step. And then they live again in the telling, when we shape those moments into myth. *Echoes of Forsaken Paths* is one such myth – a story of crystals and caves, of rivalries and revelations, but most of all, of companionship forged in peril.

The world of Thaloria remembers what people forget. And sometimes, the faintest echo of a forsaken path is enough to awaken an entire legend.

JPS Nagi
September 29, 2025
Portland, Oregon

ACKNOWLEDGEMENTS

First, I want to thank **Tony**, who was the first to act on my endless questions about role-playing games. He created my very first character, set up a session, and gave me a glimpse of what awaited beyond the dice. He also had to roll back that character's strength once he realized he'd accidentally made me a walking fortress – a "tank" who could bulldoze half his carefully designed encounters. That first session was chaos, laughter, and imagination in its purest form and it hooked me for life.

To everyone who sat around our RPG table – **Robert, Chris, Michael, Audryana**, and my daughter **Khushi** – thank you. You brought life to every moment and turned stories into shared adventures. The memories we built together – both the triumphs and the disasters – became the foundation for the worlds I now write.

To **Dhruv** and **Pankaj**, my friends and brothers, who have always supported me quietly but unwaveringly, thank you for your faith and patience – even when I disappear into imaginary worlds for days at a time.

To **Alfonso**, my *ink-and-pen brother* in both life and story – thank you for constantly urging me to write more, for reading my drafts, challenging my ideas, and reminding me that storytelling, like art, is a craft best shared.

And finally, to **Gitanjali**, who has listened to more of my half-told tales than anyone should have to and who often fell asleep halfway through them – thank you. Your quiet presence and belief in me are what let me keep dreaming, even when the words come slowly.

This book, like all stories worth telling, is the sum of many voices. I'm grateful to all of you for lending me yours.

CONTENTS

P

Prologue

efore the roads were cut through the Ashenwood, before Breezewood's banners flew proud above its walls, there was only the land, and the land was alive with music. The people of old believed that every stone carried a voice, that the roots of mountains and the veins of crystal beneath them were threads of a vast instrument tuned by the hand of creation itself. When the wind moved across peaks, when rivers carved their beds, when thunder rolled in the distance – these, they said, were not accidents of nature but chords in the world's great song. Few could hear it clearly. Fewer still dared to answer.

One who dared was a mage called Tenebros. He was not born to greatness; no crown blessed his brow, no destiny marked his path.

What he lacked in pedigree, he made up for in hunger. Where others heard the crystals hum faintly in the hills, Tenebros heard promise. Where others marveled at their beauty, he saw tools. He descended into a cavern where the veins grew thickest, a place that pulsed like the heart of the world, and there he began his work.

The stories say he forged a relic unlike any other: a Heart of crystal, vast and flawless, cut to magnify not only sound but intent. In its facets he poured his will, his fears, his desires. With it, whispers became commands, and commands became law. He raised no armies, yet soldiers marched. He lit no altar flames, yet priests bent the knee. He was but one man, and yet his voice filled the land like a storm fills the sky.

For a season, his dominion seemed unshakable. Towns turned upon themselves. Neighbors distrusted neighbors. Words, amplified and twisted, bred chaos faster than swords could end it.

But the Heart of Tenebros was no passive vessel. It drank of him even as he poured into it. Power bent back upon its wielder, echo answering echo until the man himself was little more than a hollow chamber for the crystal's hunger. One night, in the cavern where it had been born, the Heart devoured its master. The land groaned, and the cavern was sealed. Those who witnessed it claimed that the very hills shifted, folding upon the cave like a wound scabbing shut.

Tenebros was gone, but his echo lingered.

Yet legends rarely end with a single voice. In the shadows of Tenebros's rise, another figure moved – a sorceress whose name was half-remembered in scraps of song: Lysara Shadowheart. She had forged her own Heart, not from ambition but from balance, a crystal meant to temper will rather than magnify it. Where his resonance was command, hers was harmony. She stood against him in those final days, not with armies but with her own shard of the world's song.

Their clash shook the land. Mountains split, rivers changed their courses, and the people swore the sky itself dimmed. In the end, Lysara's Heart was broken, scattered into fragments to keep it from falling prey to the same corruption. Tenebros's Heart, swollen with unspent power, sank into silence beneath the earth. And so the tale of the Twin Hearts passed into myth.

Generations turned to centuries. Kingdoms rose and fell. The cavern was forgotten, its name spoken only in half-fearful warnings told to children: do not follow the crystals when they sing, for they lead only to ruin.

But the land remembers what people forget.

In time, crystals began to surface again – faintly glowing shards found in plowshares, in riverbeds, in the roots of felled trees. Some were carried into shrines, where worshippers claimed their prayers were answered with unusual fervor. Others found their way into the hands of mages who felt their spells sharpen and burn brighter than before. A few were sold in markets as charms and trinkets, little realizing the danger they held.

And with the crystals came the whispers.

At first they were subtle, like half-remembered dreams. A voice urging a merchant to demand more coin than his conscience allowed. A nudge pressing a priestess to claim visions she had not truly seen. A thought, sharper than anger, planted in a soldier's mind just before he raised his blade. The whispers promised power, certainty, clarity. All they asked in return was that they be heard.

The balance that had held for centuries began to waver. Temples split. Friendships soured. Even the faithful found themselves drawn toward new devotions, shimmering with crystal light.

It is in such times that stories awaken again.

Some said the Crystal Cave had reopened, its veins once more exposed to the air. Some whispered that Tenebros's Heart still beat beneath the stone, restless in its long slumber. Others claimed that Lysara's fragments had begun to call for rejoining, seeking a hand strong enough – or reckless enough – to bear them.

And so the age turned, as it always does, not upon kings or generals, but upon the unlikeliest of travelers: a ranger who mistrusted roads, a cleric who weighed every shadow against her god's light, a dwarf whose axe and laughter were equally loud, and a young sorcerer whose dreams hummed with music older than her own name.

They did not know, when they set their feet on the path to Breezewood, that they were already walking in the echoes of those forsaken hearts. They did not know that their choices would weigh against the silence of centuries.

But the world knew. The world had been waiting. And when the song begins again, someone must always answer.

1

THE AMBUSH'S AFTERMATH

The road that wound its way toward Breezewood was older than memory. It cut through the heart of the Ashenwood Forest, a place where the trees grew tall and close, their branches woven together like fingers clasped in prayer. The canopy let through only shafts of fractured light, so that even in broad day the forest seemed caught in perpetual twilight. For travelers, the road was both lifeline and gauntlet: the safest way to cross the woods, and yet always shadowed by the dangers that lurked just beyond the tree line.

On this quiet afternoon, the forest wore its silence heavily. A silence that was not simply the absence of noise, but something deeper, as though the land itself held its breath. The four travelers moving along the road felt it in their bones, though each responded in their own way.

Kaelen Veyra, the ranger, led the company with the fluid steps of a man who trusted neither road nor wood. He had been born in the borderlands, where danger arrived unannounced, and had learned to walk as if every twig held a secret. His bow rested across his shoulder, hand never straying far from the string. His sharp eyes scanned ahead, searching for the slightest break in the forest's rhythm.

Bram Thornfist trudged just behind, dwarf-like in both build and spirit. His axe, Stonecleaver, swung lazily in one hand, but his other clutched a wineskin he had yet to open. "Too quiet," he muttered, as though the forest could hear him. "Forests should breathe louder than this. Give me the noise of a tavern any day."

Serenya Duskbane, robed in the sun-stitched gold of Solanus's faithful, walked in silence. Her lips moved with half-formed prayers, eyes lifting now and then to the fractured light that speared through the branches. She had long since learned that silence in wild places was rarely holy.

Lyraen Voss, youngest of them, brought up the rear. She let her fingers brush the bark of trees as they passed, as though listening through touch. A sorcerer's gift flickered beneath her skin, one she did not always understand, but she felt it stir now – faint and restless. Magic lived in these woods, not wild like fire but deep and old, and her heart beat faster with every step.

It was Kaelen who halted first, raising a hand. The others stopped instantly; they had learned to trust that gesture. He tilted his head, nose twitching, eyes narrowing on the faintest wisp of smoke curling upward beyond the next bend.

"Smoke," he murmured. His voice was low but commanding, the sound of a man who knew danger needed no volume to announce itself. "Not campfire smoke. Sharper. Wood and oil."

Bram sniffed the air, his wide nose wrinkling. "Burnt pitch. That's no stewpot." He rolled his shoulders, axe rising unconsciously into readiness.

"Stay alert," Serenya said softly. "This is no place for chance."

They rounded the bend – and the forest broke into ruin.

A cart lay at the roadside, blackened and sagging, its timber frame eaten by fire that had only recently died. Smoke still curled from its splintered beams, carrying with it the bitter stench of scorched grain and charred cloth. Arrows jutted from its husk like the quills of some hunted beast. The earth around it was strewn with torn sacks, shattered pottery, bolts of cloth stained by soot and ash. The scene had the violence of a storm, and yet the precision of a blade.

Kaelen knelt by the cart, brushing aside the ashes. His fingers came away slick with blood that had dried but not yet blackened. He grunted. "Hours old. No more."

Lyraen did not look at the wreckage, but above it. She felt the air hum faintly, as though the smoke carried more than fire's residue.

"Something more than arrows passed here," she whispered. "The air still remembers."

Bram kicked a broken wheel. "Raiders, maybe. Bandits bold enough to attack this close to Breezewood? Or fools who thought the Baron wouldn't notice."

Kaelen's sharp eyes moved to the mud, where heavy prints cut deep into the earth. "Not just men. Something heavier walked with them. Armored, maybe." He traced the line of prints as they veered toward the forest's edge.

Serenya's gaze was drawn to something half-hidden under the charred wreck. She knelt, lifting a scorched canvas tarp. Beneath it lay a sealed letter, its wax cracked from heat but intact enough to show the crest pressed into it: the stylized tree and intertwined roots of House Thornwood. She turned it in her hands, her voice low but clear. "Lord Eadric Thornwood. The Baron of Breezewood."

The group exchanged sharp glances.

Lyraen frowned. "A cart bound for the Baron himself? Ambushed on his road? That's not chance. That's purpose."

Kaelen straightened, sliding the arrow he had plucked from the cart into his quiver. "We have choices. We follow the tracks, risk the ambush, and maybe learn the truth now. Or we take this letter to Breezewood, put it in the Baron's hands, and let him decide what truth is worth."

"Either way," Bram rumbled, "trouble's coming."

The silence pressed close again, broken only by the faint crackle of dying embers. Then, from deep in the woods, a crow cawed – sharp, jarring, too loud against the hush. It echoed like a warning. Kaelen's jaw tightened. He looked at his companions – the cleric whose faith bound her to light, the dwarf whose axe had seen too many battles, and the young sorcerer whose power still trembled in her veins. He nodded once, a simple gesture heavy with decision.

They had stepped across a threshold.

The road behind them led to safety, to taverns and quiet lives. The road ahead led into mystery, fire, and blood. And none of them doubted which road they would take.

2

CHAOS AT THE INN

By late afternoon, the Ashenwood gave way to fields stitched with hedgerows and low stone walls, the kind of patchwork that spoke of centuries of patient hands. Breezewood rose out of that green quilt like a promise: timber-framed houses with whitewashed walls, roofs pitched against winter storms, shutters painted the cheerful blues and reds of a prosperous market town. Windbells chimed from eaves, their silver tongues catching the breeze in bright, tinkling notes. Somewhere, a baker spilled cinnamon into hot air and turned the whole street into hunger.

"Civilization," Bram Thornfist announced, shouldering Stonecleaver as if it were a walking stick. "Which is to say: beer."

"Two days," Kaelen said without looking at him. His gaze kept moving – rooftops, shadowed alleys, the pattern of foot traffic. He had a soldier's habit of measuring safety by where danger might hide. "We deliver the letter and learn what we can."

Lyraen Voss slowed to watch a whirligig of colored glass spinning over a stall of cloth. A small girl caught her eye and stuck out her tongue; Lyra grinned and lifted a hand, making a spark dance between her fingers before she snuffed it. The child's eyes widened into delighted saucers.

Serenya Duskbane paused beneath the gilt sun-wheel mounted over a crossroads shrine. She touched her fingers to her brow, lips moving through a brief prayer. "Let your light be truth," she murmured. "And let us remember the difference."

The press of the market drew them onward: a barrelman rolling kegs with the deftness of a juggler; a pair of shepherds arguing sheep prices with a weaver; a peddler hawking amulets strung with pale green stones that glowed faintly even in daylight. Lyra felt a tickle of resonance from those trinkets – weak but real, like the echo of a distant bell. Crystals again. A theme threading through the day.

They came at last to a square centered on a stone well carved with vines. On one corner stood a building whose sign left no ambiguity about the services within: a red dragon reared on its hind legs, mug aloft, froth spilling in painted foam. The letters beneath were burned deeply into oaken plank: THE DRUNKEN DRAGON INN. Music drifted through the leaded windows – lute and hand drum, a merry air that rode the fragrance of onions and stewing beef.

"Smell that?" Bram asked no one in particular, reverent. "Stew and ale and poor decisions."

"Information first," Kaelen said, but his mouth twitched at the corner. "Then stew."

They stepped off the cobbles toward the door just as the world tore itself open with light.

A flash – white, rimmed in violet – punched through the inn's windows and shattered the street into silence. For a heartbeat Kaelen saw only afterimages: a snowfield, a corona, the shadow of his own bow. People yelled – one long, rising thread of panic – and the lute inside cut off with a sound like a throat closing.

Bram was already moving. He hit the door shoulder-first; the hinges, stout as they were, chose cooperation over resistance. The party spilled into a room that stank of ozone, scorched wood, and spilled ale. The common hall had been torn by a brief, furious storm: a table cracked in two as if cleaved by an invisible axe; a chair driven into a wall so hard its legs were embedded to the cross-brace; the reed mat before the hearth charred to a spiderweb of blackened threads.

In the center of the chaos stood two figures.

One was a young man in a scholar's coat gone to rags, the cuffs singed and eyes far too large for his face at the moment. He clutched a scroll in one hand and a thumb-sized crystal in the other that still held a sullen ember of violet light. Beside him stood an elf as tall and still as a cypress, robes dark as mid-river and embroidered in sigils that pulled at the eye if you looked too long. Silver hair fell around his face in a waterfall; his gaze, when it lifted, was a clean, sharp green.

"I did say," the elf remarked to the young man in a voice made for quiet rooms, "that taverns are poor laboratories."

The inn's staff was a half-breath from panic. A woman with flour on her apron clutched a ladle like a cudgel. A red-faced man with a mop wielded it like a halberd. Behind the bar, a dwarf with a braided beard and a chest like a barrel planted his meaty hands on the wood and boomed, "Everything's fine!" – in the universal tone that meant nothing was fine. He pushed a tray of earthenware mugs toward the crowd. "First round's on the house! Second round's also on the house, provided you put the house back together!"

The tension wobbled, then cracked. Laughter hiccuped out of someone like a popped cork. The room exhaled.

Kaelen, who had moved without thinking to interpose himself between the lightning and his friends, lowered his bow a fraction. "What happened here?"

The elf inclined his head, minimal and precise. "A lesson, interrupted." He did not apologize; he did not explain. He had the air of a man who believed both were indulgences. "Eldrin Shadowmantle, of the Arcane Circle. My apprentice, Tobin Quickspell. And you are...?"

"Travelers who prefer their stew not flambéed," Bram said, eyeing the scorch mark fanned out from the hearth like a black flower. "Bram Thornfist, at your service – so long as service includes ale."

"Kaelen Veyra," Kaelen said, still scanning for unseen threats.

"Serenya Duskbane. Lyraen Voss."

Lyra's attention had locked on the small crystal in Tobin's hand. Even guttering, its light tugged at her like a tide. The air around it vibrated at a note she did not hear so much as feel in her teeth. "Where did you get that?" she asked softly.

Tobin swallowed. "From – well, from – "

Eldrin lifted two fingers and the young man's babble sheathed itself. "From a source that requires care. More care than was exercised just now." His gaze slid to Lyra, cool and appraising. "You feel it."

"Yes," Lyra said, surprised and slightly annoyed by the honesty of her own voice.

"Good," Eldrin said, and it might have been approval or merely notation. "Then perhaps you are also capable of restraint."

Serenya moved through the room with the economy of a field healer, setting a hand on a burned forearm here, a rattled shoulder there, soothing by presence as much as by word. The scorch across the reed mat made her eyes narrow. Magic uncontrolled was not simply messy; it was often immoral in its disregard. "If your lessons threaten lives, Master Eldrin," she said, "perhaps your classroom should be stone and silence."

A beat, and then – unexpectedly – Eldrin's mouth twitched. "We agree, priestess."

The dwarf behind the bar chose that moment to vault his bulk over it with surprising grace. "Bramble Stoutbeard," he said, offering his hand to each of them in turn. "Innkeeper, host, catch-of-all-manner-of-flying-objects. My apologies for the light show. We allow music, merriment, and the occasional arm-wrestling match, but we draw the line at spontaneous indoor thunderstorms."

"Reasonable policy," Kaelen said.

"Enforceable, too," Bramble added, patting a cudgel hung cleverly under the bar. "Now – rooms, drinks, and a corner where delicate conversations can pretend they're private."

They took the corner. The inn's noise resumed around them in layers: the scrape of chair legs reclaimed from shock; a lullaby of spoons against bowls; someone re-tuning a lute that had lost its courage. Outside, Breezewood's bells marked the hour with a slow, measured dignity, as if to remind everyone that towns endured even what they did not understand.

Eldrin placed the violet crystal on the table between them. Up close, Lyra could see narrow seams within it, as if filaments of light had been frozen mid-flight. The thing pulsed faintly, not with heat but with intention.

"This," Eldrin said, "is one of many. They have appeared with increasing frequency around Breezewood and, if my correspondents are to be believed, farther afield. Some are inert, like stones more beautiful than useful. Some – " he inclined his head toward the charred reed mat, " – are less so."

Kaelen reached toward it, then checked himself, palm hovering just shy of touch. "It has the smell of a pattern."

"Of a source," Eldrin corrected, and in that moment Lyra thought he might recognize the hunger in her – this compulsion to name things truly. "Patterns are symptoms. Sources are causes. I prefer to treat causes."

"Then say the word," Bram said. "Because I'm hearing a wizard talk his way around a wizard problem, and that generally means someone else ends up with scorch marks."

Eldrin considered him, then nodded – as if deciding the dwarf had earned more than a riddled answer. "There is a place called the Crystal Cave. Old as the first stories people told themselves to make sense of night. Its veins run deep beneath these hills. Once, it was thought sealed and its echoes damped. And yet – " he tipped his chin toward the crystal, " – here we are."

Lyra's mouth had gone dry. She had dreamed of a place like that – the pressure of a thousand unheard songs pushing against her skin; light like breath caught in glass. The dreams had been fragments, slipping away on waking like fish into reeds. Hearing the words now felt like the click of a lock.

Serenya folded her hands. "If there is danger to the town, speak plainly. The Shrine of Solanus does not turn from duty."

"Nor does the Circle," Eldrin said. "But the Circle is small, and suspicion grows quickly when robed men begin sealing wells and locking doors. Better a handful of capable strangers who can move without stirring old fears."

"Flattering," Bram said. "Also accurate."

Eldrin's gaze returned to Lyra. "Tomorrow, come to the Arcane Circle at the Verdant Grove. There is history to share, and a decision to make."

Kaelen studied him. There was a weight to the elf that he knew from commanders who had lost as often as they won – men who did not waste words because they had measured what words cost. "We'll be there," Kaelen said.

Bram lifted a mug that had appeared as if summoned by his thought. "To decisions made after stew," he proclaimed, and Bramble, passing by with a tray, gave a solemn nod.

Lyra watched the crystal's last ember fade. Even dulled, it seemed to listen, like an ear turned to a door. She tried to ignore the way it tugged at her – tried and failed. Somewhere beneath the floorboards of this town, beneath its tidy streets and painted shutters, the land hummed with old music.

And somewhere not so far away, in stone veined with light, something was calling her by a name she had not yet learned to admit she owned.

3

THE ARCANE CIRCLE OF THE VERDANT GROVE

Morning came bright and clean after the inn's upheaval, a kind of clarified light that made colors ring a little truer. Breezewood's market woke like a choir in parts: first the clink of shutters, then broom-bristles scratching stone, and finally the rolling chorus of hawkers staking their patch of air. The four set out before the square filled, cutting through lanes where dew still stitched spiderwebs into silver diagrams and ivy lifted heart-shaped leaves to drink the sun.

The Verdant Grove lay at Breezewood's north edge, where the town remembered it had been forest first. Hedges gave way to shoulder-high ferns. Oaks rose with the self-assurance of elders, their roots swollen into knotted bastions. Birds kept to the understory, bright needles of sound that pricked and vanished. A path – not paved but persuaded – led toward a tower that did not so much stand in the grove as grow from it.

The Arcane Circle's tower was round and old. Its stones wore lichens like a scholar's robe wears dust. Vines climbed where carved sigils allowed them, avoiding other glyphs as if they, too, understood boundaries. A weather vane at the peak shaped like a nine-pointed star turned slowly in a wind none of them could feel.

"Wizard places always look like they've been thinking too long," Bram decided, eyeing the runes with an expression that mixed suspicion and respect. "Stone starts to brood."

"Stones remember," Serenya said, fingers grazing the low wall. "Some memories are worth brooding on."

Before Kaelen could knock, the tower's oak door swung inward of its own choosing. Cool air rolled out – book-scented, lavender-edged. Eldrin Shadowmantle waited within, sable robes uncreased by either haste or sleep. Tobin lingered behind him with the attentive awkwardness of a student trying to be less present than he was.

"Welcome," Eldrin said, and somehow made the single word both greeting and assessment. "This way."

They followed him through a helical stair that wound around a hollow core. The inner shaft opened onto rooms like petals around a stem. Some were study-cells; others, laboratories with stoppered glass and armillary spheres and chalk diagrams halfway to proving or disproving something important. The building hummed – not audibly, but with the taut, invisible music of wards set carefully and woven tight.

Eldrin brought them to a circular chamber where light fell from a high oculus and pooled on a table of black wood. Shelves climbed to the ceiling, crowded with books that had known several hands and arguments. In the center of the table sat a crystal the size of a hen's egg, caged in a silver gimbal that allowed it to tilt and spin. Even inert, it insisted on being noticed.

Tobin cleared his throat. "Tea?" he blurted, then flushed, then produced a tray as if to overtake his own embarrassment. The tea was delicate and grassy; it steadied without dulling, a kindness disguised as a beverage.

Eldrin didn't sit. He stood with his palms on the table's edge, head lowered a fraction, as if addressing both them and the crystal at once. "What you saw yesterday," he said, "was a symptom. It is time you understood the cause."

Kaelen nodded once. "We prefer causes."

"Good." Eldrin flicked two fingers; the silver gimbal spun. The crystal within answered by waking – a soft internal warmth that climbed quickly to a throat-sung hum. It shed no heat. It shed intention. Lyra felt the note like a finger drawn down the bones of her forearm.

"These are Veinsong crystals," Eldrin said. "Most folks know them, if at all, as trinkets: pretty stones that sing when struck, or catch light like bottled dawn. Their true nature is rarer – and more dangerous. In certain configurations, they do not merely echo sound; they amplify it. Not just sound, but resonance: prayer, command, rage, desire. Give them the right lattice and a song becomes a shout, a whisper becomes a will."

Bram blew out a breath. "And your apprentice tried to whistle a thunderstorm."

Tobin's ears went a politically inconvenient shade of red. "It was an extremely minor test," he muttered. "On a very modest lattice."

"Modest lattices are for modest minds," Eldrin said mildly, which might have been a reprimand or a proverb. He rotated the gimbal again; the crystal's hum shifted, harmonizing with something beneath the floor. "The crystals keep appearing in markets and pockets. They should not. Not unless the source – "

" – has reopened," Lyra said, the words arriving so certainly that she startled herself. A dream unfurled at the edges of memory: light like breath caught in glass; a pressure behind the eyes as if a chorus waited for permission.

Eldrin's eyes met hers. For the first time a distinct emotion moved behind them – satisfaction tempered by caution. "Yes. We kept its name out of coin-speech for generations, believing it safer as rumor than as map. But you may as well hear it from a more honest mouth. The Crystal Cave lies a day's walk into the hills. It was sealed after... events that should not be footnoted."

Serenya folded her hands, thumb rubbing the ridge of a burn-scar that had long since lost its heat. "Why was it sealed?"

"Because people are worse than pressure," Eldrin said, so dryly that Bram barked a laugh. Then the elf's voice lowered. "Because a mage – call him Tenebros, though names grow moss – sought to bend the Cave's veins to his will. He made a heart for his purpose, and the land obliged him until it broke him in return. We closed the mouth and damped the echoes. The hills slept."

"Until now," Kaelen said.

"Until now," Eldrin agreed. He gestured and Tobin set a rolled chart on the table. When he opened it, the ink itself glimmered faintly, lines of lay threading like rivers. "Crystals have been surfacing – smuggled, stumbled upon, sold as charms. People call them blessings. Others call them omens. Meanwhile, tempers fray. Petitioners at the Shrine of Solanus come away angrier than they arrived. The Crystal Temple rises on a tide of certainty. This is not politics, though it will wear politics like a mask. It is resonance. It is pressure returning to a system not made for it."

Serenya's jaw tightened. "If devotions are being warped, the Shrine must act."

"The Shrine must be seen to act," Eldrin said. "But if priests and mages posture publicly, Breezewood divides itself by reflex. I would rather send four strangers to ask the one question none of our factions will: what is happening under our feet?"

Kaelen's response was the thought already in him, set to words. "You want us to go to the Cave."

"I want you to go and come back," Eldrin said, gaze steady. "Alive, with knowledge. If the Cave is merely bleeding off history – broken veins finding new paths – we can stanch and suture. If it is waking..." He let that word hang like a bell's aftertone. "Then we will require a different kind of courage."

Bram scratched the braid at his chin. "And if we find your Tenebros down there asking for his heart back?"

"Then," Eldrin said, "you will wish you had eaten two breakfasts."

Tobin made a helpless noise that might have been either a suppressed laugh or a swallowed groan. He stepped to a side shelf and brought back a small, velvet-lined box. Inside lay a crystal not unlike the one in the gimbal, but flatter, cut into a lens held by a ring of dark metal. Unlit, it was beautiful. When Lyra's shadow fell across it, the lens woke with a candle-thin thread of gold.

"A compass?" Kaelen asked.

"A conductor," Eldrin said. "It does not point toward the Cave so much as agree with it. Near the mouth, it will sing. Inside, it will attempt to make choices for you. Do not let it."

Lyra hesitated, then reached. The moment her fingers touched the metal ring, she felt a gentle tug in her chest, as if something had found the note of her marrow and plucked it. The lens brightened a fraction, a pulse like a heartbeat without body.

"It likes you," Tobin said, both wonder and warning in the words.

"Tools don't like," Kaelen said automatically. But he watched Lyra's face the way he watched storm-fronts.

Eldrin turned to Serenya. "You will need to name your light every hour you are below. Not to keep darkness away – it belongs there – but to keep it honest. Darkness lies when left alone."

Serenya inclined her head. "Truth is the sun's first language."

Eldrin faced Bram. "Everything down there will want to ring. Your axe will ring, your armor will ring, your bones will ring. You must strike as if sound is a weapon, because it will be."

"Always has been," Bram said, and for a breath the room contained a different dwarf entirely, younger and standing amid the clamor of a siege-line, learning that war is a kind of music.

"And you," Eldrin said to Kaelen, "must continue to see what others miss while everyone else is listening too hard." He unfolded a second chart – this one a simple relief map of the hills north-east of Breezewood. "There's an old shepherds' path to a retired quarry. From the quarry's far wall, follow the water's talk. When it grows quiet where it should be loud, you are near."

"Water's talk?" Bram asked.

"Streams chatter over stone," Eldrin said. "When their song dims for no reason, something is swallowing the sound."

They stood a moment in the chamber's pooled light, the work of leaving pressing in on all the things they did not yet know. It felt to Kaelen like the breath a bowman takes between sighting and loosening – a pause that contains both caution and commitment.

"What do we owe you if we return empty-handed?" Kaelen asked.

"An honest account," Eldrin said. "And, if you can afford it, the humility not to make a story where there is only mystery. People will be eager to turn your uncertainty into prophecy. Deny them."

Bram closed the velvet box with a soft click. "Stew first," he suggested, because someone had to say something human. "Then we'll go meet your sleeping problem."

Eldrin's expression softened by a degree. "There is bread here. And cheese that does not shame itself." He nodded toward a sideboard, as if reluctant to admit hospitality lest it grow into expectation. "Eat. Then take the side path out of the grove; it keeps you off the main road. Fewer eyes. Fewer ideas about who you are."

Lyra slipped the lens-compass into her satchel and felt, absurdly, as if the bag were now heavier with more than weight. The tower's wards murmured as they retraced their steps. At the threshold, Eldrin spoke once more.

"Remember," he said, the words light but landing with the authority of a seal, "the Cave will offer you the courtesy of reflecting what you bring it. Choose your thoughts as you would your weapons."

Serenya touched the sun-disk at her throat. "And if we are offered a choice without a right answer?"

"Then choose the answer you are willing to be," Eldrin said, and the door swung wide to give them back to the bright, ordinary morning.

Outside, the grove breathed. The town's bells marked the hour. Somewhere far beyond both, under hills that hid their secrets like pearls, a song older than the road cleared its throat.

The four looked at one another, and the decision, already made, simply acquired a direction.

4

THE CRYSTAL CAVE

he hills northeast of Breezewood were not welcoming. They rose sharp and sudden out of farmland, their slopes covered in scrub and thorn, their peaks jagged as broken teeth. Old shepherd paths twisted across them, faint tracks where hoof and boot had pressed for generations, but the way was not kind. The sun set early in these hills, its light caught by the cliffs so that afternoon wore the shadow of evening.

The four made steady progress, the silence between them marked not by unease but by a shared purpose. Kaelen led with a scout's instinct, finding traces of old quarry routes and dry streambeds that cut narrow seams through stone. Every so often he paused to press fingers into the earth, to listen for what he could not yet see. His silence spoke volumes: the air was too still, the bird-song absent. They were heading into a place the living no longer claimed.

The compass crystal guided them with an almost petulant will. At Lyraen's touch, it pulsed faintly, dragging her steps toward valleys and ridges she would not otherwise have chosen. The closer they followed its call, the more the land itself seemed to resist. Sound dulled here – streams whispered instead of chuckled, the wind moved but refused to sing in grass or tree. Even Bram, usually quick with complaint, noticed it. "Feels like walking through the back of a cathedral," he grumbled. "Hallowed, but not holy."

They descended a final slope into a hidden valley. Mist pooled at its floor, white and restless, curling in slow tides. The cliffs encircled the valley like a stone crown. At its center yawned the mouth of a cave, half-hidden by moss-hung rock. From that dark throat, the silence was complete. The compass in Lyra's hand blazed with a steady golden thrum. None of them needed words: they had found it.

Serenya spoke a prayer softly, her voice steady though her eyes betrayed unease. "Light reveal only what we can bear."

Kaelen scanned the valley rim. No smoke, no camps, no carrion birds. Either no one had come this way, or no one had returned. He notched an arrow, testing the pull of his bow. "Once we cross that line," he said, nodding at the cave mouth, "we're not on the road anymore."

Bram spat into the mist. "Road's overrated." He hefted Stonecleaver onto his shoulder and strode forward.

Inside, the world changed.

The first breath was damp and cold, but clean, like water drawn straight from a mountain spring. The second was filled with vibration – a hum not heard but felt, the resonance of stone itself alive. Then came the light. The walls and ceiling were veined with crystal, their facets glowing with a ghostly radiance. They refracted each other's beams until the chamber shimmered like the inside of a giant jewel. Every step sent echoes cascading, sounds that multiplied and returned, weaving together into an uncanny music.

Lyraen pressed her hand to the wall. The crystal's song leapt into her, a thousand notes overlapping, words half-formed in forgotten tongues. She staggered, Serenya catching her arm. "It's speaking," Lyra whispered. "Not to me, but through me."

"Keep focus," Kaelen said sharply. "The cave wants your thoughts more than your steps."

They advanced cautiously along a glassy path that wound between colossal crystal spires. The air seemed thicker here, heavy with unspent intention. Shadows bent strangely, light scattering in prisms that made the path shimmer and shift. Even Bram's steady boots faltered once, his muttered curse swallowed by echoes that turned it into a chorus.

Then came the grinding.

Ahead, a spire detached itself from the wall. At first it seemed simply a rockfall in motion, but then the pieces realigned, limbs unfolding, a torso resolving. The thing stood twice a man's height, a construct of faceted crystal held together by light. In its chest glowed a core, bright as molten gold. The Crystal Golem moved, each step ringing like a struck bell, vibrations rattling their teeth. Bram grinned, though his eyes were tight. "Finally. Something I understand."

"No," Kaelen hissed. "Not here. Sound is its weapon – every clash will make it stronger."

They ducked between pillars, moving in silence broken only by the golem's resonant steps. Each time its head tilted, the prisms of its face refracted dazzling rainbows that painted the walls, threatening to disorient. Pebbles betrayed them once, tumbling down a slope. The golem turned with deliberate inevitability, the cave itself amplifying the strike of its footfalls.

Kaelen led them on a weaving path, gestures sharp and economical. At one point he pressed them flat against a spire as the golem passed close enough for the hum of its body to vibrate through their bones. Lyra clenched her fists to keep her own magic from answering the resonance – a struggle that left her breathless.

At last the path opened into a great chamber. Here the crystal formations converged, casting light into a heart-shaped monolith taller than any of them. Its glow was warm, golden, almost gentle compared to the harsh brilliance around it. Unlike the rest, it did not hum. It pulsed, slow and steady, like a heartbeat too vast to belong to flesh.

They knew without speaking: this was the artifact. The Heart.

Lyra felt it calling her, not in words but in rhythm. Each pulse synchronized with her own breath, her own blood. She took a step before she realized she was moving. Kaelen's hand on her shoulder halted her, but she could not look away.

"Careful," Serenya whispered. "Even holy light can burn."

The hum rose, and for the first time words coalesced within it. Not one voice, but many, weaving in dissonant chorus.

In shadows deep and truths untold, lies a tale of hearts grown bold. Seek not afar but look within, for the foe you fear wears a kin's skin.

Lyra's knees weakened. She clutched the satchel at her side. "It's... it's speaking prophecy."

Bram's hand tightened on his axe. "Never liked poetry."

Kaelen scanned the walls, listening as fractures spidered out across the chamber. The cave was not still anymore. It was waiting. Testing. Judging.

"Whatever we do," he said, voice taut, "we do it fast."

5

THE HEART OF THE CAVE

The chamber seemed alive, a cathedral sculpted from crystal and sound. Columns rose like frozen lightning, their facets scattering the glow of the heart-shaped monolith at the center. The hum pressed against their skulls, a choir too vast to comprehend. Every breath felt borrowed, every movement judged.

Kaelen scanned the walls, his eyes narrowing at the spiderweb fractures racing across some of the larger spires. "This place is listening. Careful what you give it."

Lyraen could barely hear him. The Heart called her forward, each pulse of its golden light syncing with the rhythm of her veins. She reached unconsciously toward it, only to feel Kaelen's hand close around her arm.

"Not yet," he said. His voice was tight but calm, the voice of a man speaking on a battlefield where silence could mean survival. "Look first. Touch later."

Bram grunted, setting Stonecleaver's haft against the floor. "What's to look at? It's a rock. A bloody pretty rock, but still a rock."

"No," Serenya said. Her gaze lingered on the Heart's glow, her face shadowed by both awe and worry. "It's alive. Or near enough to alive. And alive things demand respect."

They approached the base of the Heart cautiously. There, almost hidden by the glow, lay a lattice of smaller crystals, each a different hue. They were arranged like a flower, their tips angled toward the monolith as though in reverence. When Kaelen brushed one lightly with the flat of his blade, a single, clear note rang out, echoing through the chamber. The Heart's glow brightened in response.

Serenya inhaled sharply. "It's a lock. A hymn waiting to be sung."

Bram crouched, tapping a thicker crystal with his knuckle. The resulting tone was deeper, resonant, and sent a tremor through the floor. The lattice shifted, rearranging slightly. The Heart pulsed brighter.

"Or," Bram muttered, "it's a trap."

Lyraen knelt, eyes wide. "It's both. A puzzle made of resonance. The right harmony opens it. The wrong one... well, the cave will let us know."

Kaelen grimaced. "So we play the right song. Quickly."

They began cautiously. Serenya tested notes with her voice, each hum harmonizing or clashing with the lattice. Kaelen tapped his dagger gently against certain shards, his archer's precision finding tones true. Bram struck with the haft of his axe when deeper notes were needed. Lyraen listened, her sorcerer's senses attuned to the ebb and swell, guiding them when they strayed close to dissonance.

At first, the sound was chaos – a jumble of echoes colliding. But slowly, painfully, it coalesced. A melody emerged, haunting and strange, as though the cave itself remembered a song sung in its bones long before men built towns. The Heart pulsed brighter, each beat matching the harmony more closely.

Lyraen's hair clung to her damp forehead as she leaned into the final note. Her hum rose pure and clear, threading through the others like sunlight piercing mist. The lattice responded. The petals of crystal unfolded in a radiant bloom, revealing a narrow gap at the base of the Heart.

Kaelen exhaled. "That's our door."

The golden light spilled outward, bathing Lyraen's face as she stepped forward. Her hand trembled as she reached for the Heart. The hum became a whisper inside her skull – no words, only the sensation of welcome and recognition, as though the Heart had been waiting for her all along.

She whispered a spell, coaxing the stone free. The Heart shifted, loosening from its cradle as if it had chosen to release itself. It hovered for a breath in her hands, impossibly light for its size.

And then the world broke.

The hum erupted into a roar, shaking the chamber so violently that shards cracked and fell from the ceiling. The Crystal Golem, forgotten in the echoes behind them, reawakened. Its steps rang out like war drums, faster now, drawn by the disturbance. The cave itself groaned, fractures racing across the walls like veins of lightning.

"Move!" Kaelen barked.

They sprinted, the Heart cradled in Lyraen's arms. Every step triggered fresh cascades of shards from above, glittering rain with the sharpness of knives. Twice Bram flung himself over the others, Stonecleaver deflecting chunks of crystal that would have shattered bone. Serenya called the light of Solanus to her palms, forming radiant shields that splintered falling shards before they struck.

The Golem loomed ahead, its jagged form blocking the narrow choke-point that led back to the surface. Its chest blazed with molten light, the sound of its core vibrating the very marrow in their bones.

Kaelen loosed an arrow, not at the Golem but at the ceiling above it. The shaft struck true, splitting a weak point in the crystal. A cascade of heavy shards thundered down, burying the construct in its own cathedral. The impact echoed like a funeral bell.

"Go!" Kaelen shouted, pulling Lyraen forward.

They hurtled through the choke-point, the path trembling beneath their boots. The light of the entrance flared ahead, mist and freedom calling. The cave groaned once more, a sound like stone in agony. The ground buckled, pitching them forward. They tumbled out into the valley just as the cave's mouth collapsed in a thunderous avalanche, a cloud of dust and glittering shards billowing outward.

Silence followed, but it was no longer the silence of waiting. It was the silence of an ending.

For a long moment, they lay gasping on the valley floor. The Heart pulsed softly in Lyraen's arms, its light golden and steady, as if nothing had happened at all.

Bram rolled onto his back, laughing breathlessly. "So... that's it? We nearly get buried alive, and we end up with a glowing rock?"

"No," Serenya said quietly, her eyes fixed on the artifact. "We began something. And I fear it won't end with us."

Kaelen sat up, scanning the cliffs, already calculating their way back to Breezewood. "Then we'd better start preparing for what comes next."

Lyraen clutched the Heart tighter, the whisper of its rhythm still inside her. It was more than a relic. It was a promise. And promises always had a cost.

6

RIVALRIES IN EVERSPRING

he path away from the Crystal Cave wound down into gentler hills, but the weight they carried made every step heavier. Lyraen bore the Heart in a satchel against her chest, and though the artifact was light as glass, she felt its steady pulse in her bones. Every few steps it seemed to echo with her heartbeat, as if it were trying to braid itself into her life. She said nothing of it, though the others could see the hollowness in her eyes.

"Keep it close," Kaelen said once, not unkindly. His gaze never left the horizon. "But don't let it decide for you."

Everspring appeared by midafternoon, a town unlike Breezewood in both shape and spirit. Where Breezewood was a place of trade, noisy with wheels and coin, Everspring was devotion and bloom. Its name proved no lie: flowering vines spilled over walls, gardens blazed in color, and little springs leapt through the cobblestones like silver threads stitching the streets together. People smiled here, but not idly – theirs was the confidence of those who believed their gods were close enough to touch.

Yet even before they reached the square, the tension in the air was palpable. The crowd in the market was drawn tight, eyes flicking between two departing figures. One was a woman in green robes embroidered with curling vines, auburn hair loose around her shoulders. Around her neck hung a teardrop crystal that glowed faintly even in daylight. The other was an older man in the sun-stitched gold of Solanus, his long white beard lending him gravity. The two had clearly just exchanged words – words sharp enough that the silence left behind was brittle.

"Not shouting," Bram observed under his breath. "That's worse."

The two parted in opposite directions, leaving the onlookers buzzing like bees around a disturbed hive. Kaelen caught a passing fruit seller by the arm. "Who are they?"

The woman glanced about, wary of ears. "Priestess Liora of the Crystal Temple," she whispered, "and Elder Harbin of the Shrine of Solanus. They used to be friends. Now they speak only to disagree."

Serenya's lips tightened. "Solanus is my god. If his shrine is torn by strife, I must hear why."

They didn't need to seek answers. Answers came to them.

A boy in a blue tunic approached, clutching a folded note sealed in wax. Ink stains marked his fingers. "For you," he said nervously, thrusting the note at Kaelen before scampering off. The seal bore the mark of Everspring's mayor.

Inside, the letter read simply: Mayor Elmond requests your presence. Mediation is needed.

Elmond's home overlooked the central square. The man himself was broad-shouldered, his hair silvered but his eyes sharp. He welcomed them with practiced warmth, but his smile did not hide his weariness. He poured spiced tea into clay cups, the steam rising between them like incense.

"You've arrived at a moment of delicate balance," Elmond said. "Everspring has always been two devotions in harmony – Solanus, lord of the sun, and Arvina, lady of growth. We held festivals together, prayed together, grieved together. But balance is fragile. Now the Crystal Temple rises on one side, the Shrine of Solanus grows defensive on the other, and I stand in the middle watching the ground split."

He gestured toward the satchel in Lyraen's lap, his eyes lingering on the faint golden glow leaking from its seams. "And then you arrive with a relic that could tip the balance entirely."

Kaelen didn't flinch. "You want us to hear both sides."

"I want you to see both sides," Elmond corrected. "They'll tell you what they believe. It will fall to you to decide what you believe."

The Crystal Temple stood half-built but already dazzling. Its walls were inset with luminous stones, and its windows were angled to scatter light into prismatic rainbows across the unfinished floor. Workers carried scaffolds and polished gems, but they moved reverently, as though each hammer-strike was part of a hymn.

Priestess Liora welcomed them with open arms and a smile that radiated certainty. "I know what the Shrine says," she told them as she led them inside. "That we seek power. That we corrupt devotion. But what we build here is not in opposition – it is expansion. The crystals are Arvina's gift to her children, to remind us that nature's beauty can hold divinity."

Her hand brushed the teardrop crystal at her throat. Lyraen felt the answering pulse from the Heart in her satchel and had to bite her lip. The resonance was undeniable.

"Elder Harbin calls it corruption," Liora continued, her smile faltering only a breath. "But is it corruption to embrace what the land freely offers? Or is it fear of change that drives him?"

Serenya bowed politely, though her expression was storm-gray. "Truth does not change," she said. "Only our understanding of it."

Liora's smile did not waver. "And what if the truth is larger than we imagined?"

The Shrine of Solanus was simpler, a stone pavilion open to the sky, crowned with a great golden disk that caught the afternoon light and flung it back across the square. Worshippers knelt in neat rows, their voices raised in prayer that blended into a low, steady chant. The air here smelled of incense and sun-warmed stone, comforting and familiar.

Elder Harbin greeted them with respect, though suspicion clouded his eyes when he saw Lyraen's satchel. "I have no quarrel with Arvina," he said, his voice measured. "But I know these crystals. They were sealed away for good reason. They amplify not only what is good in us but also what is dark. I see it already – ambition sharpened into pride, faith twisted into zealotry. Priestess Liora's devotion is true, but I fear she no longer commands it. It commands her."

Serenya's jaw clenched. "If Solanus's faithful are being bent, we must resist."

Harbin nodded. "Resist, yes. But resist wisely. If the crystals gain the town's full heart, Everspring will not be Everspring anymore."

That night, they gathered in their rooms above the inn. The Heart sat on the table between them, its glow soft and insistent. The conversation from both temples lingered like smoke in the air.

"Two leaders," Kaelen said, "both claiming truth. One of them might be right. One of them might be lying. Or neither."

"Or both," Bram countered, crossing his arms. "I've seen men tell the truth so hard it turned into a lie."

Lyraen stared at the Heart, her hands clenched in her lap. "What if it's not about them? What if it's about us? About me?" Her voice cracked on the last word, and the others fell silent.

Serenya reached across the table, laying her hand gently over Lyraen's. "Then the choice will still be yours. Relics don't make people. People make choices."

The Heart pulsed once, golden light brushing their faces like a silent answer.

7

THE SHADOWED ENCHANTRESS

The forest northeast of Everspring was older than its hills. Oaks towered like cathedral pillars, their roots swollen into ridges that split the ground. Mist clung low, thick enough to blur edges into suggestion. No birds called here, no squirrels scurried. Even the wind seemed reluctant to trespass.

"This place doesn't breathe right," Bram muttered. He swung Stonecleaver lightly, as if the weight of the weapon could anchor him against the strange hush.

Kaelen knelt briefly, touching the moss. "No tracks. Not even deer. Something keeps them out." He rose and nocked an arrow, his eyes hard. "Stay sharp."

The compass crystal in Lyraen's satchel pulsed brighter with each step. She felt it tug at her ribs like an insistent hand. She wanted to ask if the others heard the hum in the air, but she already knew the answer. This music was hers alone.

They followed a narrow path through twisted undergrowth until it opened into a clearing unlike any other. The trees bowed inward, their branches braided into a living archway. At the center stood a woman.

Her presence struck them before her voice did. She was tall, her black hair gleaming like polished obsidian, her robe a deep violet stitched with constellations in silver thread. A sheer mantle drifted around her as if borne by currents invisible to the rest of the world. She carried no staff, no blade, yet the grove thrummed with her power.

Kaelen raised his bow. "Name yourself."

The woman's gaze passed over him as though he were a detail in a painting, before settling on Lyraen. Her lips curved into a smile that was both kind and knowing. "You already know my name."

Lyraen's throat tightened. She did not, and yet – she did. The whispering voice that had haunted her dreams since the Crystal Cave rose up within her. The name slid into her mind like a memory that had been waiting. "You're... the Shadowed Enchantress."

The woman inclined her head. "Lysara Shadowheart. To most, a villain from old stories. To you... kin."

The word landed like a blow. Lyra staggered back. "Kin? That's impossible."

Lysara extended her hand, palm open. Resting there was a pendant shaped like a silver flame. Lyra's breath caught. She had owned one exactly like it as a child, found among the few belongings of the mother she had never known. She had thought it lost forever.

"I gave you mine the day you were born," Lysara said softly. "When the choice to raise you was taken from me."

Serenya stepped forward, her sun-disk catching faint light. "What game is this? Speak plainly."

"No game," Lysara said, her voice carrying the weight of truths too heavy to lie. "My blood runs in her veins. I have watched her from afar, waiting for the moment when the world would call her to choose."

Bram spat into the moss. "And now you come striding out of the shadows to claim her? Sounds like a trick."

Lysara's smile faltered into something sharper. "Believe what you will. The Heart she carries does not lie. It is Lysara's Heart – my heart – broken and hidden long ago when the world was not ready for balance." She turned her gaze on Lyra again, and for a moment, all her power seemed softened by something close to tenderness. "And now the balance must be restored."

Kaelen's bowstring creaked as he drew it back. "And if we refuse? If this is just another sorceress trying to play gods with people's lives?"

"Then you will learn too late," Lysara said simply. Her mantle stirred as though in a breeze none of them felt. "The Heart of Tenebros is waking. Its shadow already stretches across Thaloria. When it rises fully, your blades, your prayers, even your courage will be as kindling against a storm."

Lyraen's voice trembled. "Why me?"

"Because you are both key and counterweight," Lysara said. "You carry my blood, and you hold my Heart. Only through you can the two hearts – mine and Tenebros's – be joined and silenced forever. But know this: such a joining comes at cost. You will not leave unchanged."

Silence spread, heavy and close. The mist curled tighter around the clearing.

Serenya was the first to speak. "You ask her to carry the weight of an entire world."

"I ask her to fulfill what she was born to do," Lysara corrected gently. "We cannot choose the song we inherit, only whether we sing it true."

Bram stepped forward, squaring his shoulders between Lyra and the Enchantress. "Songs, hearts, destinies – it all sounds like a tale told to frighten children. I know one truth: no stranger takes her without going through us."

Lysara's smile returned, sad and knowing. "And so loyalty binds you. Good. She will need it. But remember – loyalty can sharpen into chains if you cling too tightly."

The Heart in Lyraen's satchel pulsed, hard enough to make her wince. She pressed a hand to it and felt her own heartbeat stutter into its rhythm. She thought of the dreams she'd had all her life: the crystal chambers, the whispers in forgotten tongues, the sense of being chosen without consent. Now, in the Enchantress's presence, the dreams no longer felt like riddles. They felt like truth.

Kaelen's arrow stayed nocked, but his voice was measured. "If you want her to trust you, then tell us where this leads. What must be done?"

Lysara's gaze swept across them, settling on the forest's far edge where the trees grew darker, their trunks twisted as though in silent agony. "Beneath the ruins of Breezewood's first temple lies the Heart of Tenebros. When the stars align, it will awaken fully. If that happens unopposed, the land will suffer a tide of corruption from which it may never recover. Only by uniting his Heart with mine – with her – can the balance be restored."

Lyra's voice was a whisper. "And if I fail?"

Lysara's answer was as soft as falling ash. "Then all of Thaloria falls with you."

8

THE DEADLY RELIC

The ruins of Breezewood's first temple crouched in a grove of yew and elder, stones bowed by weather and roots. Moonlight made a patient ledger of the place: arches reduced to ribs, pillars gnawed to nubs, a floor pried apart by green insistence. Long ago, people here had believed their prayers climbed these columns like vines. Now only wind and memory kept vigil.

Kaelen paced the perimeter, a shadow skimming slower shadows. He traced old lines with a hunter's touch: the seam where a flagstone had been lifted and replaced, the scrape marks of a hinge along an iron-bound edge half-sunk in moss. "Here," he said quietly, and knelt. He brushed centuries of lichen aside to reveal a trapdoor fused into stone by rust and neglect. A ring sat in a recess, sealed by a thin thew of iron.

Bram wedged Stonecleaver's flat beneath it and leaned. Metal protested, then yielded with a hiccuping cough of flakes. The ring rose. Beneath the door's lip, runes glimmered – not the bright etch of fresh warding but the embers of something old that still remembered it had a purpose.

Serenya bent, her breath a steady cadence. "Rite-seal, sunward keyed, layered with a counterpoint," she murmured. "This temple married light to law."

Lyraen touched the runes and felt them answer with a whisper of cool understanding. The Heart in her satchel pulsed in her palm like a bird trapped and beating. She swallowed and drew her hand back. "It recognizes me," she said, not in pride but in the shame of unearned inheritance.

Together they worked – Kaelen spotting the false sigil among true strokes, Bram steadying the door's weight so it wouldn't scrape and wake whatever listened, Serenya shaping a low chant that turned the old locks toward obedience, Lyra easing a breath of power where the pattern needed it. The runes sighed. The seal unwove. The door opened upon a stair whose breath had never known the taste of sun.

"Down is the only way left," Bram said, humor for courage's sake, and they descended.

The air cooled rung by rung. Moss gave way to stone, stone to a kind of carved darkness that drank light without malice. Their lantern's glow seemed to cling close, reluctant to stray from their hands. The hum they had come to recognize as the land's deep music returned, not the polyphony of the Crystal Cave but a slower, heavier tolling – as if a bell were being rung beneath the world by a giant made of patience.

The stair unspooled into a hall vast enough to hold the memory of a city. Pillars stood like arrested storms, their surfaces banded with veins of crystal shot through with threads of dull gold. At the far end, above a dais of black stone, something hung in air – a heart-shaped crystal floating as if the laws of the room were looser than the ones above. Within it, molten gold sluiced slowly like sunlight trapped in thorns. Each pulse flexed the hall's light, making shadows breathe.

The Heart of Tenebros.

Lyra's mouth filled with metal. Not taste – memory. The memory of the Crystal Cave's hum, the golem's tolling steps, the moment the earth decided to shift. But here it wasn't resonance that frightened her. It was purpose. This Heart didn't sing. It decided.

Lysara Shadowheart stepped from a side arch as if darkness had poured and settled into a woman. The violet of her robes seemed to be the color the rest of the world had given up to make room for night. "You came," she said, voice quiet, but in this hall quiet did not mean small.

Kaelen set himself between Lyra and the Enchantress without thinking. "You set the stage," he said evenly. "Don't pretend to be surprised we walked onto it."

"I am not surprised," Lysara said. "I am... warned. Anything could be a choice this close to a heart."

Serenya's eyes never left the floating crystal. "What must be done."

Lysara gestured to the dais. "The lattice Tenebros built remains. He forged a chamber to magnify will. Mine broke on it. His curdled inside it. The ritual is simple and terrible: bring the Hearts together, bind them with equal measure, and bid them fall silent." Her gaze settled on Lyra. "You carry the measure."

"Equal measure," Bram repeated. "Meaning what, exactly?"

"Meaning," Lysara said, "she must ask both halves to be what she is. If she is unbalanced, so will the world be."

Lyra stepped forward before her courage could look about for arguments. The others moved with her, a constellation around a star that might yet decide to collapse. The Heart in her satchel thrummed like a struck string, answering the low tolling of Tenebros's core. She drew it out.

Lysara's breath caught - not a performance, but a memory unguarded. "I split it to keep the land whole," she said, almost to herself. "And now the land asks to be mended by my blood."

Kaelen angled his head. "And if the Hearts devour the hand that holds them?"

"Then grief will become a language we all learn," Lysara said. Her eyes met Lyra's. The power in them softened. "You do not owe us your life. But the world will spend it anyway if you refuse."

Lyra lifted the golden Heart. Her hands shook, but not from weight. "If I do this," she asked, "do I become you?"

Lysara flinched, the first crack in the porcelain poise. "No. You become what you choose in the moment you choose it. That is all any of us have ever been."

Serenya's fingers brushed Lyra's wrist, a silent prayer poured into touch. "Name your light," she said. "Not what others called you. What you call yourself."

Lyra nodded, and stepped onto the dais.

The Hearts felt each other the way weather fronts do – long before they touched, the air thickened, the pressure rose, the hall's stones shrank and swelled with invisible tides. When the distance closed to a hand's breadth, the lantern guttered and died. Light came from the crystals themselves, a tawny glow from Lyra's and a colder gilding from Tenebros's that made edges too sharp to be safe.

"Begin," Lysara said, and her voice had the cracked beauty of a bell that's been asked to ring beyond its casting.

Lyra raised her chin. "I am Lyraen Voss," she said, and the hall listened. Even the tolling paused. "I am not your blood's mistake nor its redemption. I am the choice I make now."

She brought the Hearts together.

There was no collision, no shattering. The crystals met and passed into each other like two notes struck to make a third. Light flared – white at first, then colors Lyra knew she would ache to remember and never quite manage. A shockwave cracked the surface of the dais and sent fissures racing out to the pillars. Kaelen staggered and set his body against Lyra's as if mere bone could argue with this magnitude. Bram roared a wordless defiance from a throat born to resist caves closing. Serenya's prayer became music, then meaning stripped past sound, then simply presence.

Lyra was nowhere and everywhere. The Hearts were a lens and she was the eye pressed to it. The world rushed through the smallness: a thousand small angers sharpened into blades by crystals worn at the throat; a thousand prayers heated to zeal by windows that turned sunlight to command; a thousand griefs given a song too loud to weep beneath. And under it all the first music, the earth's long patience, wanting only to go on.

"Equal measure," she whispered, though she had no mouth. "Be what I am."

What are you? the Hall asked – not in words, but in the test pressure always applies to a vessel.

Lyra thought of a child touching bark to listen for sap. Of a girl stealing fire from her own hands because it felt like a secret shared instead of a punishment. Of a woman standing beneath a sky that never asked permission and realizing permission was the last name of fear. "I am a listening," she said. "I am a refusal. I am a promise that has not decided what to promise yet."

The Hearts quivered against her definition. One wanted to command. The other wanted to cradle. She held both urges lightly as if they were birds and not laws, and in that lightness found purchase. "Fall silent," she said, and gentleness carried farther than force could have.

The light imploded. Sound pulled inward as if the room inhaled to become smaller than breath. When the world returned, Lyra was on her knees. In her open palm lay a spark no bigger than a tear. It glowed gold without burning. The vast Hearts were gone.

The hall exhaled. A small rain of dust fell from somewhere out of sight. Then the first stones shifted.

"Time to no longer be here," Bram said, all business now that the miracle had chosen not to argue.

They ran, guided by the dim insistence of the spark in Lyra's hand and the remembered geometry of panic. Behind them, the hall sloughed history with methodical groans: pillars giving up, vaults shrugging loose. Twice Kaelen shouldered a fallen lintel just enough to slide people under it. Once Serenya's light turned a shower of crystal into harmless ash. At the stair, the world tried to remember how to be earth and sky at the same time. They chose sky.

They came up under a moon higher than the one they had left and a wind that seemed shocked to find them breathing in it. The ruins had shifted. A new crack ran like a black river through the nave. Owls called, because owls have the good sense to be late.

For a long time, they said nothing. The spark warmed Lyra's palm like proof of something she might not be ready to name.

Lysara climbed from darkness a moment after them, her poise broken to a more human geometry. Her hair was loosened from its perfection. Her eyes were a storm remembering the sun behind it. She looked at Lyra's hand and an expression moved across her face that might have been grief made gentle. "You did not become me," she said, relief and loss braided inseparably.

"No," Lyra said, voice hoarse. "I became the choice I made."

"Which is how not to become a legend's mistake," Lysara replied. She took a step back, mantle stirring. "My work here is done. The land will carry the rest." She looked as if she wanted to say more – something soft and unlearned – but what she had been for centuries could not shape the words. She inclined her head to each of them – Kaelen first, for distrust honestly given and therefore worthy; Bram next, for loyalty with a spine; Serenya, for light without contempt; Lyra last, because the last word is often the truest – and turned to go.

"Will I see you again?" Lyra asked, surprising herself with the ache of it.

"When the world asks a question that needs both shadow and mercy," Lysara said without turning, and was gone into trees that accepted her as if they had been keeping a seat.

They did not march triumphant into Breezewood. Triumph felt like a word that belonged to people who had not been under the world while it tried to be more than it could carry. Still, the town met them at the gates in a tide: the Baron whose seal had crossed their path at the beginning; Mayor Elmond with his careful eyes; Bramble Stoutbeard with a tray already stacked with mugs; half the market and all the children. Everspring sent representatives by morning: Priestess Liora with the light from her necklace dimmed to something more honest; Elder Harbin with fewer edges on his certainty.

Serenya stood in the square where both devotions had contended and told the truth they could bear. "The crystals remain," she said. "But their loudest voices are quiet. If you wear them, wear them as beauty, not as law. If you pray through them, pray to your gods, not to your fear."

Harbin bowed, not to her but to what the words made possible. Liora bowed back, and for the first time their gestures made a bridge instead of a wall.

That night, the Drunken Dragon Inn remembered how to be exactly what it was for: laughter too loud, stew that forgave the day, a lute that missed two notes and made up for it with heart.

Bramble raised a mug and roared a toast that mispronounced all their names on purpose so he could pronounce the last word clearly: "Friends!"

Kaelen slipped to the door and stood for a while on the threshold, a ranger measuring the difference between inside and out. He felt a weight lift that was not the absence of danger but the presence of decision. When he turned, the room met him with the uncomplicated warmth of people who had decided they were better for you having come back.

Bram arm-wrestled a blacksmith and lost graciously. "You had the table," he said solemnly, as if it were a rules clarification. The blacksmith laughed until tears cleaned his face.

Serenya repaired a scorch mark on the reed mat near the hearth with needle and thread, the small work fitting the day's large mercy.

Lyra sat at a quiet table and opened her hand. The spark hovered above her palm, not rising, not falling, as if it trusted her enough to rest. It was not power, or not only. It was the memory of a choice made under the hill, a promise to be the person who had made it. She closed her fingers around it and felt it settle like a heartbeat that had decided to keep time with hers for a while longer.

Eldrin arrived late, robes road-dusted, expression uncharacteristically unshielded. He listened to the shape of their account rather than the words, as mages do when they are honest about what matters. "You have done more than you know," he said at last. "The loudest changes do not always make the lasting ones."

"Will it hold?" Kaelen asked.

"For a time," Eldrin said. "And time is the only gift that lets people become worthy of their stories."

Outside, the wind moved through Breezewood's signs and set the windbells chattering. The town answered like a house with many rooms whose doors had all been opened. Somewhere in the distance, the hills exhaled, and the old music returned to what it prefers: a hum so steady most never notice it, which is how you know a thing is truly alive.

They slept that night not as heroes but as people who had done a difficult thing as well as they could. In the morning, the road would be there, as it always is. It would offer them choices, as it always does. And they, changed but still themselves, would decide again and again who they were willing to be.

The world, for now, went on.

E

EPILOGUE

Spring came early to Thaloria that year.

In Breezewood, the air smelled of thawed earth and blossoming orchards. The market thrummed with voices, no longer sharpened by suspicion but softened by trade and laughter. The Shrine of Solanus and the Crystal Temple still stood on opposite sides of the square, their banners bright in the wind. But where once they had drawn lines, now they found ways to braid them. On feast days, worshippers carried both sun-disks and crystal pendants, walking side by side. Balance had not been restored fully – it never is – but it had been remembered. And remembering was enough.

At the Drunken Dragon Inn, Bramble Stoutbeard told the story of the cave's collapse with his usual liberties. Each retelling grew more spectacular: Kaelen's bowstring became fire-forged steel, Bram himself single-handedly held the roof of the cave, Serenya's prayers rang like bells that shattered stone, and Lyra – always Lyra – glowed like the sun reborn. The patrons cheered, mugs lifted high, knowing well enough that truth was smaller than the telling, but happier for the larger tale.

Kaelen Veyra did not correct them. He had never been a man to crave legend. Still, when he walked the town's walls and looked to the horizon, he felt something had shifted. The land carried fewer shadows than before, though shadows would always return. He kept his bow close, not because he mistrusted peace, but because he knew it was fragile.

Bram Thornfist, for his part, drank, laughed, and sparred as though life had always been this generous. Yet at night, when the fire burned low, he polished Stonecleaver in silence. He had heard the cave's resonance deep in his bones, and he knew war was not the only thing that rang loud. Some nights he caught himself humming the melody of the crystal lattice, and though he cursed when he noticed, he could not quite stop.

Serenya Duskbane divided her time between the Shrine and the Temple, a bridge where once there had been a wall. She spoke often of truth as light, but she also spoke of shadow – not as enemy, but as necessary contrast. Her faith had not changed, but it had deepened, like a river cutting its bed a little lower. She prayed not just for protection but for wisdom, knowing now how easily devotion could be turned.

And Lyraen Voss… she was no longer the girl who had left Breezewood with only questions. She was not yet the woman she would become, but she had taken the first irrevocable steps. The spark in her palm still glowed, faint but alive, a reminder of the Hearts joined and silenced. It whispered nothing, offered no prophecy. It simply waited, a mirror to her choices.

Sometimes she feared it. More often she wondered if it was not a burden but a seed.

One night, under a sky heavy with stars, Lyra walked beyond the walls to the edge of the Ashenwood. She held the spark aloft, and for a moment it flared, answering some deep harmony in the land. The trees did not bow, the earth did not quake, yet she felt seen – not as chosen, but as acknowledged. She closed her fingers around it and breathed easier.

The Shadowed Enchantress was gone, but not gone. Some said she had dissolved into mist, her work complete. Others claimed she still wandered the hidden places, waiting for the next imbalance to stir. Lyra did not know which to believe. Part of her hoped their paths would cross again. Part of her feared they already had.

And so the four companions remained in Breezewood a while, their names spoken kindly in markets and taverns, their deeds already stretching into the fabric of story. Yet the road beyond the town still called. The world was wide, and its music did not end with one cave or two Hearts.

Kaelen watched the horizon, Serenya watched the people, Bram watched for the next tankard, and Lyra watched her own hand with the spark that glowed there. Different watches, same company.

When at last they set their boots on the road again, there were no fanfares, no banners, only the steady rhythm of footsteps and the knowledge that stories rarely end. They only pause, waiting for the next verse.

And in the silence between heartbeats, if one listened closely enough, the land of Thaloria still hummed – a song of stone and shadow, light and choice, always waiting for those willing to answer.

C

MEET THE COMPANIONS

Every story begins with a road. This one began with four travelers who did not intend to walk it together. Fate, it seems, is less a plan and more a collision.

Kaelen Veyra – The Watchful Ranger, Human

Kaelen has the look of a man who counts exits before entering a room. Years spent along Thaloria's borderlands taught him that survival belongs not to the strongest, but to the most observant. Once a soldier in a forgotten war, he now makes his living as a guide — though his true calling is caution.

He trusts few, speaks little, and keeps his pain folded neatly between his silences. The forest bends to his will not out of fear, but respect. To his companions, Kaelen is the steady hand and wary heart — the one who sees the trap before it's sprung, and still steps forward when the others cannot.

Serenya Duskbane – The Voice of Solanus, Half-Elf Cleric

Where Kaelen watches for danger, Serenya listens for truth. A cleric of Solanus, the god of the sun, she carries her faith like a lantern through shadow — steady, unwavering, but not blinding. Half-elf by birth and bridge by nature, Serenya moves between worlds: mortal and divine, doubt and belief.

Her calm is not the absence of fear, but the mastery of it. When she prays, her words do not rise — they settle, like warmth into cold stone. In Everspring, where temples war beneath banners of light, her presence reminds others that faith without compassion is only another kind of darkness.

Bram Thornfist – The Axe and the Ale, Dwarf Warrior

If Kaelen is the blade's edge and Serenya the balance, Bram is the heartbeat that keeps them moving. A dwarf with a voice that could shake tavern rafters and a laugh that could resurrect a tired soul, Bram is as quick to joke as he is to swing his axe, Stonecleaver.

He hides his grief behind good ale and louder stories — a veteran of sieges that left more scars than medals. Yet beneath the bluster lies loyalty so fierce it borders on sacred. When Bram fights, it is never for glory, but for the person standing beside him. In every battle, he reminds the others that courage and joy are kin, and that laughter is sometimes the only weapon that cuts deeper than fear.

Lyraen "Lyra" Voss – The Dreaming Sorcerer, Elf

Lyraen's power came long before her understanding of it. The youngest of the four, she carries within her a raw, untamed magic — the kind that hums even when she sleeps, whispering of places she has never seen. Her dreams are haunted by crystal light and the echo of a mother's voice she cannot remember.

Naïve and brilliant in equal measure, Lyra balances wonder with recklessness. She questions everything — the gods, her companions, the world itself — but her heart is fiercely kind. In time, she will learn that her magic is not a gift of chance, but of lineage, and that her greatest enemy may not be the one who stands before her, but the shadow of the blood that binds them.

Individually, they might have survived. Together, they might yet save something greater than themselves. Theirs is not a company of destiny or prophecy, but of chance — a ranger seeking redemption, a cleric chasing balance, a dwarf defying despair, and a young sorcerer born of light and shadow.

And when the road bends toward danger, as it always does, they will discover what all companions eventually learn: that every echo begins with a single voice willing to be heard.

About the Author

JPS Nagi resides in the picturesque Pacific Northwest, where towering evergreens and misty mornings shape both his days and his imagination. He shares life's adventures with his wife, two children, and their spirited Maltese dog, Snowy – named after Tintin's faithful companion.

JPS finds joy in exploring new ideas, playing board games, and, more recently, diving deep into the boundless worlds of role-playing games. These passions fuel his storytelling, inspiring tales where chance, choice, and imagination converge.

When not writing fantasy adventures, he curates his personal blog, Planet Nagi, a constellation of musings (Soliloquy) and original stories (Inked Orbits) that reflect his love for words and the many worlds they create.

www.PlanetNagi.com